by the same author

ALPHONSE, THAT BEARDED ONE

HORTENSE

THE COW FOR A QUEEN

Natalie Savage Carlson

ILLUSTRATED BY *Nicolas*

HARCOURT, BRACE AND COMPANY, NEW YORK

LIBRARY OF CONGRESS CATALOG CARD NUMBER: 57-5537

PRINTED IN THE UNITED STATES OF AMERICA

For Dan

1.

Once upon a long time ago, Louis XVI lived in a big palace in France with his wife, Marie Antoinette. And a brown and white cow named Hortense lived in a village near a castle in Normandy.

Hortense was a motherly peasant cow who had never pretended to be anything she was not. She had raised three calves and raised them well.

Two of them were in the same herd with her. But her first-born—her beautiful white calf—had been taken away.

Hortense could not understand this. She often tried to find the calf. She once wandered up to the castle on the hill because she had seen the calf led away in that direction. She looked through the kitchen garden, but the cook drove her away. She looked in the formal garden, but the gardener drove her away. She looked in the rose garden, but the Countess herself drove her away.

9

From then on, she faithfully stayed with the herd. She munched grass in the green pasture that lay along the great sleeve of the sea that the French call *La Manche*.

All the cows chewed their cuds, waved the switches of their tails, and thought about making milk. But Hortense chewed her cud, waved the switch of her tail, and thought about where her lost calf might be.

One green spring day, as Hortense was waving the switch of her tail, she chewed her cud so hard that she chewed a brand-new thought out of it.

Perhaps her calf was hidden in the willow thicket that sheltered an inlet of the sea near the end of the pasture. That is where the calf had been born. Perhaps it was there waiting to be found again.

Hortense chewed this over in her cud for a long time. She shook her horns and stared dreamily at a ship anchored on the sleeve. A cow never acts hastily. If she did, she might knock over her bucket of milk or fall into a ditch.

The sun was dipping into the sea before Hortense decided to do anything about her thought. Soon the cowherd would appear to drive the herd home. If she wanted to look in the willow thicket this day, she must start on her way.

So Hortense shook her horns and wriggled her pinbones.

She slowly picked her way to the thicket that lay at the edge of the water. She tried to keep herself from going too fast lest she sour her milk.

The thicket looked deserted, but a cow always has hope. That is why she goes on making milk as fast as it is taken from her.

Suddenly Hortense's soft brown eyes saw a movement in the thicket.

"Moo," she bawled happily, because now she was sure her long-lost white calf was waiting among the willows. She waved the switch on her tail. She shook her horns and quickened her cloven hoofs.

But alas for the hope that grows in a cow's great heart! Two fierce-looking men leaped out of the willows at Hor-

tense. They had bandannas tied around their heads, and golden rings hung from their ears. Worst of all, they brandished sharp cutlasses.

"Moo," bawled Hortense, because she was a motherly Norman cow who had never known violence.

The men glared at her fiercely. Then they dropped their cutlasses and laughed.

"A cow," said the fat one.

"Nothing but a cow," said the other, whose nose could slice cheese.

And what did they expect to see in a Norman pasture by the sea? A hippopotamus?

"Moo," bawled Hortense, who had expected to see a white calf instead of two ruffians.

"Why not a cow?" asked the fat one of his companion. "Why not tripe and stew and oxtail soup instead of that endless salted beef?"

The man with the sharp nose shrugged his shoulders. "You are smart, Jean the Fat," he said. "And her horns would make a pretty pair of powder horns. I like the way they curve."

So the fat one took hold of one of the pretty horns and led Hortense into the thicket.

"Moo," bawled Hortense, because she thought the kind men

were leading her to her lost calf.

They led her to a new surprise instead. In the inlet of the sea was a boat filled with casks of water. A third man was filling a last cask from the stream that lost itself among the willows.

"A cow," he said also. "Did Philippe the Daring tell us to get a cow, too?"

"Of course not, Jean the Stupid," said Jean the Fat.

"Will we hold her for ransom?" asked Jean the Stupid.

"No," answered Jean the Fat. "We will make her walk the plank."

"We shall give her a boat ride anyway," said the man whose nose could slice cheese.

So the three of them helped Hortense into the boat—which was not an easy task because a cow is not built for sailing. But into the boat went her head and her hoofs and her pin-bones. Only her switch did not go into the boat. It hung into the water.

"Moo," bawled Hortense with delight, because she knew she was going somewhere and that was where her calf must be.

The three men sat down and began pulling at the oars. The boat left the willows and floated over the great sleeve of water that the English call *The Channel*. On that green spring evening a long time ago, it seemed to belong to the ship with high-riding decks and tall masts.

"Moo," bawled Hortense with greater delight, because no one had ever thought to take her for a boat ride before. She had been into the castle gardens and all the way to a fair once, but she had never been in a boat.

The small boat soon reached its mother.

There is something else that had never happened to Hortense before. She had never been hoisted into the air by ropes looped around her body. The small boat fell from under her hoofs. She dangled in the air. Up, up, up went Hortense toward the high deck.

"Moo," she bawled unhappily, because she was beginning to distrust the men and because her hoofs and tail felt so heavy.

Jean the Fat and Jean the Stupid scrambled up a rope ladder. The sharp-nosed man waited below in the little boat.

Hortense was sprawled across the railing and flopped onto the deck. She was quickly surrounded by a group of untidy men.

"Moo," bawled Hortense, because a cow who has been robbed of her dignity has nothing left her but night and day.

Everyone stared at Hortense as if she had come from above instead of below. Then a great, blustering man came rushing down from the poop deck. He looked even fiercer than the others. He wore a red turban on his head and a red sash around his middle. The curly black hair of his beard grew anyhow and every which way.

"A cow," he bellowed. "How did this cow get aboard the *Blue Moon?*"

Hortense liked him immediately. His voice and eyes

reminded her of her father.

"Moo," she bawled back in a friendly way. She shook her curved horns and returned his stare with her soft, brown eyes.

Jean the Fat tried to explain. "Stew and oxtail soup, Philippe the Daring," he said. "We have not had any for so long."

"And her tail would make a good fly swatter," said Jean the Stupid.

"Moo," bawled Hortense pleadingly to Philippe the Daring, because she did not want to be any of these things.

Her eyes were soft, her voice moving, and her whole manner gentle and well raised.

Philippe the Daring rattled his cutlass. "Simpletons!" He

scowled at the two Jeans. "Don't you know that this is a milk cow? Would you butcher your foster mother?"

No one argued with the pirate leader. One with such a fierce face and such a sharp cutlass was not likely to meet arguments often.

"From now on we shall have milk to drink," said Philippe the Daring, "like the captains of the King's fine ships."

"Moo," bawled Hortense in agreement. It was already past her milking time.

"Jean the Fat," continued the leader, "can you milk a cow?"

Jean the Fat shrugged his fat shoulders. "No," he answered, "but I can drink it."

"Jean the Stupid," said the daring Philippe, "can you milk a cow?"

"Not I," answered Jean the Stupid. "I cannot even milk a calf."

No one knew how to milk a cow.

"Back to the boat," Philippe the Daring ordered the two Jeans. "Make a raid into the nearest village and kidnap a milkmaid—and don't forget some hay."

The two scrambled down to the boat again, where the sharp-nosed man waited.

Hortense was left on deck. One of the men quickly made

a rope halter and tied her to a cannon. The others sprawled around her in a circle and licked their thick lips.

They sat there while the darkness fell on their shoulders. A dim lantern was hung in the shrouds.

"The King's ship may still be searching for us," warned Philippe the Daring. "I do not think we have lost it yet. What a chase we led them!"

From time to time he peered into the darkness. Hortense peered into the darkness, too. Her heart was heavy with disappointment, and her bag was heavy with milk. She had not found her calf. She could not even understand what it was she had found. A ship was strange to her, and men with earrings and cutlasses were never seen in her village.

How could a simple Norman cow know that she had fallen into the clutches of bloodthirsty pirates?

There was great excitement when the small boat returned with the two Jeans and the man whose nose could slice cheese. It returned with someone else also, someone as new and strange to it as Hortense.

A woman was dragged aboard the *Blue Moon*. She looked like a very noble woman. Her red velvet cape was lined with fur. Her curled headdress was almost as tall as a dovecot. The panniers of her skirt were stiff and full. Hortense recog-

nized her as the Countess who had driven her from the rose garden.

Philippe the Daring held a lantern high to look at her. He saw not a frightened woman but a very angry one.

"Peasant!" she cried. "How dare your men carry me off like a sack of flour? I shall tell the King about this. He will have you hanged from your own yardarm."

"Ho, ho!" exclaimed Philippe. "One who wants a hare stew must first catch his hare."

The Countess tilted her nose. "You look more like a pirate to me," she said.

"You are as smart as you are beautiful," said the daring leader politely. "I am Philippe the Daring, scourge of the seven seas."

"The frogs must be very frightened of you," said the Countess.

"Moo," bawled Hortense, because not one word was being said about milking.

The fine woman peered into the shadows by the cannon. "It looks like Hortense, the village cow," she said.

"Moo," bawled Hortense, because she thought if someone did not milk her soon she would burst or die.

Her unhappy cry reminded Philippe of this. He stamped

his foot and bawled like Hortense's father. "Dolts!" he shouted. "Is this what you have brought back for a milkmaid? This bundle of pouf and fripperies?"

"We met her coach on the road," said Jean the Fat. "She must be very rich."

"So we thought we could hold her for ransom," said the sharp-nosed man.

"Perhaps she can milk a cow, too," said Jean the Stupid.

"Idiots!" roared Philippe. "Who is going to milk the cow?"

"We brought back some hay," said Jean the Fat quickly. "We found a bag of it tied under the coach for the horses."

"Moo," bawled Hortense for absolutely the last time.

The pirate leader shrugged his shoulders in despair. "Show the prisoner to a cabin on the poop deck," he ordered. *"I will milk the cow. I was once a country boy. But the first man to laugh gets twenty lashes of the cat-o'-nine-tails."

The grand Countess was led away to the poop deck. Hortense was milked by a daring pirate, and no one laughed. And early next morning the King's ship appeared on the horizon, so the *Blue Moon* sailed away.

2.

The pirate ship sailed far away from Normandy. And, of course, Hortense had no choice but to sail away with it. No one asked her what she wanted to do. But that was not unusual. What cow has ever been asked if she would rather lay an egg than give milk? Or if she would rather ride to pasture in a coach than upon her own cloven hoofs?

Hortense gazed across the sleeve of water that opened to the great sea. She gazed upon the sea that grew bigger and bigger. She watched the King's ship grow smaller and smaller. She watched the land shrink into nothing.

She tried to understand, but she asked no questions. She did not have to ask questions because the Countess was asking them all for her.

"Where are we going?" she asked in her noble rage. "Why are you taking me to sea when I have agreed to be ransomed? Is this old shoe of a boat seaworthy? Who will fix my hair?

What are we going to have for supper?"

She asked these questions of every pirate who came her way. She was very bothersome.

"Moo," bawled Hortense, as if to say, "That last question is the first one in my mind."

Nearly every pirate gave the same answer to all the questions. "You will have to ask Philippe the Daring," each one said.

But Jean the Stupid and Jean the Fat said, "Why didn't we leave you in your coach? If only someone could answer that!"

And all the while the strong winds were blowing the *Blue Moon* down to the coast of Africa.

Philippe the Daring was trying to hide from the Countess. He had so many troubles already. The new man they had kidnapped in Marseille had turned out to be a miller instead of a pilot. There were weevils in the flour, and the water was running out. And the King's ship was catching up with them again.

As if this luck was not bad enough, Philippe found himself stuck with a scolding woman and a cow that had to be milked twice a day.

And, of course, the scolding woman knew where to find

24

him twice a day. "Aha, so you are hiding under the cow's tail again," she cried, leaning over Hortense's gentle horns.

"Where else would I be found at milking time?" asked Philippe the Daring. He was doubly unhappy because he was sure that the woman's husband would pay no ransom for her. Perhaps he would have to pay the Count to take her back.

The Countess clasped her panniers, which were quite wrinkled by now. "So you are supposed to be a pirate?" she

asked. "I have seen braver stableboys. Why do you let the King's ship chase you over the sea like a frightened warren rabbit? Why don't you turn and give battle? I have never seen a sea battle. It might be an amusing story to tell the Queen."

Philippe the Daring hung his head. "It is so simple that even a cow could understand," he said. "The King's ship carries thirty-two cannon, and I have only eight."

"Moo," bawled Hortense, because she hadn't understood anything since she had blundered into the pirates in the willow thicket.

"Coward!" sneered the Countess.

"There are more old cowards than old heroes," Philippe reminded her.

So because the pirate wanted to live to be an old coward instead of a dead hero, the *Blue Moon* sailed down the coast of Africa.

Hot winds blew from the shore. A hot sun shone down on the decks of the pirate ship. Sand boiled in the rolling waves. The coast was barren and hilly.

Food and water began to grow scarce. Everyone was put on rations. The pirates measured the water they gave to Hortense. Then they measured the milk that she gave to them. They did not want to be cheated.

Each day they made plans to put a boat ashore to get provisions and water. But each night they were frightened out of their plans, for the sea was full of flames. Such a sight had been seen by few of the men—certainly not by the miller of Marseille.

"We must be near the land of the Moors," said Jean the Stupid. "Their sorcerers have set the sea on fire to frighten us away."

"Nonsense!" exclaimed Jean the Fat who had sailed these waters before. "It is only the phosphorus in the water that glows like fire at night."

But the pirates shook their beards and their earrings. They refused to believe the fat one. Everyone had heard of sorcerers, but who had ever heard of an element that shone like fire in the dark?

At last there was no water, so soon there would be no milk. And if the milk stopped, surely there would be no Hortense. The pirates were licking their lips and talking about beef stew and headcheese and oxtail soup.

Everyone became so hungry and so thirsty that Philippe the Daring decided to chance a landing on the wild shore.

Hortense watched the land come closer. Oh, this must be where her calf was waiting! Perhaps these kind people were making the trip to take her to her calf. She tugged at the rope that held her to the cannon.

"Furl the sails!" cried the pirate leader. "Wet the anchor!"

Soon the men swung out the small boat. Hortense tugged at the rope that held her captive. Surely they would take her ashore with them.

But alas! There was only disappointment in store for the cow. Jean the Fat and Jean the Stupid and the man with the nose that could slice cheese climbed into the boat. Philippe handed each one a pistol.

"And if you don't find something to eat," he ordered them, "don't come back. That will be three less mouths to feed."

"Moo," bawled Hortense, because there are sorrows so deep that only a cow's moo can express them.

The Countess went to Hortense and stroked her white brow. "We must stick together," she said, "because we are the only women in this world of men."

"Moo," bawled Hortense again, because she thought the men had made a very poor world of it.

Everyone waited uneasily for the boat's return. All the pirates looked at Hortense. Some of them took out their cutlasses and began sharpening them.

Three shots were heard beyond the rocky hills.

"They have shot something," said one pirate hopefully.

"Probably themselves," said another.

At his words, the pirates moved closer to Hortense. She chewed her cud and moved the switch of her tail and wished they would give her less attention.

Late in the evening, the boat party returned. The three men were singing gaily. The small boat was filled with casks of fresh water. And they hadn't shot themselves. The man with the sharp nose had shot an antelope, and the two Jeans had shot the sky.

There were even bags of salad greens for Hortense. Never had pirates seized such rich bounty. It was more precious than the treasure in the chest of Philippe the Daring.

"Pooh!" cried Philippe, gnawing a roasted antelope

30

haunch. "Who wants a chest of jewels when he can have roast antelope?"

"Moo," bawled Hortense. She would have chosen hay any day.

"Never at the King's feasts have I tasted such delicious meat," declared the Countess. She daintily licked her white fingers and rubbed them on her panniers.

Hortense nosed into an open sack of salads. If only her white calf—yummy, what a delicious flavor! Chomp, chomp, chomp went her grinders. As her three stomachs filled with food, she began to feel more hopeful. It is easier to hope on a full stomach. Hoping on three full stomachs makes one quite overjoyed.

Tomorrow would be a happier day. She would surely find her beautiful white calf tomorrow. And until tomorrow she would go on eating these delicious greens. And she did.

Next morning Philippe the Daring took a swig of milk from his mug. Then he spat it into the sea. He poured the rest of the milk from his mug into the sea. He sniffed the inside of the mug, then threw it into the sea.

"Onions!" he cried. "Onions in the milk!"

One by one the crew tasted the milk in the bucket.

"Onions," they agreed, for an onion cannot easily pretend to be something else. An egg plant or an oyster plant may pretend, but an onion is honest.

"The milk would have tasted good in the antelope gravy," said Jean the Stupid. "I thought it lacked something."

"All is not lost," said the Countess bravely. "Such delicious soup I shall make with Hortense's milk!"

Philippe the Daring was not satisfied. "Where did the onions come from?" he roared. "Who has been feeding the cow onions?"

All the pirates shrugged their shoulders.

Then Philippe the Daring questioned Hortense. "Where did you get the onions?" he asked her sternly.

Hortense was so ashamed that she hid her face in the salad

sack. The pirate pulled it away from her. He picked up a handful of the greens. He snuffled at them like a rhinoceros.

"Wild onions!" he cried, for Philippe the Daring, having once been a country boy, knew what these things did to a cow's milk in the spring. "Who gathered all these wild onions?"

"It was Jean the Stupid," tattled Jean the Fat. "He said they smelled good."

"And so they did, sir," said the trembling Jean the Stupid. "I didn't know what a cow eats, so I just pretended that I was a cow and picked the things that smelled good to me."

"Moo," bawled Hortense approvingly, because she liked wild onions very much. What cow does not?

"The menu for today is creamed onion soup," said the Countess cheerfully. "I will make it myself as I make it at the Queen's little house when we play at being peasants."

So Hortense could raise her horns again and look everyone straight in the eye. She felt that, although she hadn't found her calf, she had done a very clever thing.

3.

The *Blue Moon* was getting closer and closer to the equator. The King's ship seemed to have given up the chase, but new excitement and fear grasped some of the pirates.

From the earliest sailing days, it has been a custom for ships crossing the equator to perform a strange rite. All sailors crossing for the first time must join the Order of Neptune, King of the Deep. Oh, it is a proud thing to become a member of King Neptune's court! But it is a fearsome thing.

For days before the ceremony, frightening hints and veiled threats were made by the old wolves of the sea who had already been christened.

"Ho, ho, Jean the Stupid!" said Jean the Fat. "Wait until you get christened by King Neptune. You will wish that you had jumped into the Moors' fiery sea."

The men who had already crossed the equator sniggered into their fists and whispered among themselves. They collected odd equipment and refused to tell what would be done with it.

"We know who will play King Neptune," said Jean the Fat with a wink, "but what about his queen? We must have a Queen Amphitrite."

Hortense ate the last of her onion salad. Perhaps she was worried about crossing the equator, too, but she only shook her horns and waved the switch of her tail.

Philippe the Daring scratched his turban with one hand and pulled his beard with the other. Then he decided on the queen.

"The Countess," he decided. "It will be a promotion for her."

"Indeed I shall not," said the favored lady. "I play-act only in the Queen's theater at the Petit Trianon. And I have never seen planks that looked less like the Queen's charming stage than the deck of this old shoe of a boat."

"But we must have a queen," insisted Philippe the Daring. "What fun is a court of King Neptune without his queen?"

The Countess laughed a delightful little laugh. She tripped over to Hortense. Then she lifted her panniers (which were quite soiled by now) and dropped a stately curtsy.

"Your Majesty," she said.

"Moo," bawled Hortense, because she was a humble Norman cow who had never done any play acting.

At eleven o'clock in the morning, the *Blue Moon* stubbed

its bow on the equator and came to a stop.

"We are now directly over Neptune's palace," announced Philippe the Daring. "The King of the Deep will board the *Blue Moon* at any minute. The boat has been lowered for him."

Even Hortense was interested in the antics. Perhaps her lost calf would come aboard with King Neptune.

"Prepare the King's pool," ordered Philippe the Daring.

Immediately a great wooden tub was dragged out on deck. Pirates lowered buckets into the ocean and emptied them into the tub.

Jean the Fat mysteriously disappeared.

"The Queen," cried the Countess. "You almost forgot Queen Amphitrite."

Someone unfastened the rope that held Hortense to the cannon. The Countess laid her own velvet cape across Hortense's shoulders. A pirate sash was tied into a beautiful bow on her tail.

Philippe the Daring was so charmed with Hortense's appearance that he ordered the treasure chest brought from his cabin. He carefully lifted the lid. A diamond necklace sparkled in the hot African sunlight.

"The Queen's necklace," cried the Countess. "So this is

why Marie Antoinette never received her necklace."

Philippe the Daring grinned devilishly. "You don't think I chanced sailing *La Manche* to do nothing better than kidnap a countess and a cow, do you?" he asked.

He hung the priceless necklace around Hortense's short neck. And who could say that it did not become her as well as it might have Marie Antoinette?

"Wait!" cried the Countess. "She needs more fashion." So she jerked four false curls from her own red head and twisted them around Hortense's horns. The dishonest crimps had been straightened by the sea air, and the curls hung like frayed ends of rope, but it gave Hortense just the needed dash.

The Countess clapped her hands. "She looks like a lady of the King's court," she said. "Better than the King's aunts."

Hortense was led to the ship's railing. To her surprise, Neptune pulled himself over it to meet her. He was really Jean the Fat with a beard of seaweed and a cloak of fishnet and a boat hook for a trident.

He and his queen marched to the tub of water. A bucket was upended for his throne, but Hortense remained standing.

King Neptune shook his trident. "Now for the scoundrelly shrimps and crawly crabs and crayfish that infest this ship," he cried. "Bring the rogues before me."

"Moo," bawled Hortense, because that was her opinion of some of the pirates.

It took some time to round up the rogues because most of them had sneaked away and found hidey-holes during the preparations.

But one was pulled from the scuppers and two dragged down from the crow's nest. Three had even taken refuge in the bilges, and Jean the Stupid was found right in the treasure chest.

"Jean the Stupid," Philippe introduced him to King Neptune. "Caught stealing jewels from the treasure chest."

"On your knees before me and my queen," roared King Neptune.

Before the luckless Jean could obey, strong arms gave him a push from behind. He went headfirst into the tub. Splash, splash! He rose sputtering and coughing. The strong arms shoved his head under the water again. As he pulled his head out the second time, King Neptune demanded, "Do you believe that I am ruler of all the seven seas?"

Jean the Stupid blew the water out of his head like a desperate whale. "I believe that you're trying to drown me," he spluttered. "That's what I believe."

King Neptune was satisfied. "Spoken like a true salt," he

nodded. "Let him join my Order."

"Moo," bawled Hortense, trying to tell her royal spouse that another ship was entering his realm. But everyone was too busy with the ceremony. No one noticed the ship flying the golden lilies of another king.

Jean the Stupid was pulled out of the tub. A new rogue was dragged before King Neptune. One by one the pirate rogues were given a rough christening. Only one more was left, and no one could remember who he was.

All the pirates were so busy trying to remember who had been overlooked that they did not see the ship closing in on them.

Boom! A cannon ball hit the mast and dropped into Neptune's pool. The great splash christened everyone. King Neptune jumped to his feet, dropping his trident. He raced to the railing and dropped into the boat below.

"The King's ship!" roared Philippe the Daring. "Man the cannon!"

Some of the pirates obeyed him, and others followed King Neptune into the boat.

Boom! Boom! The bowsprit snapped, and the top of the foremast came toppling down.

"Fire the cannon!" cried Philippe the Daring, waving his cutlass.

As the cannon roared and smoke clouded the deck, Queen Amphitrite braced her hoofs against the boards and bawled. She wanted to be back in the green pasture of Normandy. She didn't want to be a queen. She didn't even want to be a cow any more.

Jean the Stupid wanted to be elsewhere, too. But before he deserted his ship, he yanked the diamond necklace over the cow's horns. He pushed it into his sash, then dived into the water. He began swimming for the boat in which the

41

frightened pirates were rowing away from their ship. He was not always as stupid as his name.

Boom, boom, boom, boom roared the King's ship to every single boom from the *Blue Moon*. There really were thirty-two cannon against eight.

In the dead silence that followed, Hortense could have sworn that she heard a rooster crow.

Boom, boom, boom! Hortense could have sworn that she heard a pig squeal.

More booms! Then Hortense knew she heard a cow moo.

It must be her lost calf. Her beautiful white calf was on the King's ship, which was coming alongside the *Blue Moon*. She started across the deck. A cannon ball went right between her horns, carrying away the false red curls. She stepped across a body that belonged to the Countess, who had fainted and was missing the battle completely.

Straight into the enemy fire walked Hortense, because a cow will go through anything for her calf.

The King's sailors came swarming over the rail. They were armed with daggers and pistols. Hortense advanced to meet them with lowered horns. She had a streak of stubbornness that went all the way from her poll to her pinbones. Nothing would keep her from her calf this time.

No one came forth to battle the King's sailors. Most of the pirates were in the sea, swimming for the boat. The Countess was still in her faint. Philippe the Daring was caught in a fallen sail as neatly as a sparrow in a net. Only Hortense was left to face the enemy.

The King's sailors did not look surprised to see a cow on the pirate ship. They were only surprised when they saw that she was wearing a velvet cape and a red bow on her tail. If only they could have seen her with the false red curls on her horns!

"A pirate cow!" exclaimed one of them. "She must have stolen that cape."

Hortense was grateful to them for helping her over the railing onto the King's ship.

"Lead her to the manger," they told a cabin boy.

"Moo," bawled Hortense hopefully. She took a last look at Philippe the Daring. He sat gloomily on the deck of the King's ship while sailors fastened his arms and legs with chains. Then he was carried down a dark hatchway. Hortense never expected to see him again.

4.

Hortense was led to the bow of the ship, where the anchor chain was worked.

First she saw the squealing pigs in their plank runway. Secondly she saw the coop of chickens. Lastly she saw a fat red cow with a dish face and haughty horns.

"Moo," bawled Hortense in bitter disappointment.

The dish-faced cow lowered her horns and shook them at Hortense.

A sailor lad put the two cows side by side. "Company for you, Madame Captain," he introduced them. "A pirate cow."

Madame Captain switched her tail disdainfully. Then she raised her left hind leg and gave Hortense a swift kick.

"Moo," bawled Hortense, moving as far away as she could. She did not kick Madame Captain back as she might have. She was a motherly Norman cow, not a pirate, and she had never taken part in violence.

Hortense quickly learned that things were run quite differently on the King's ship *Dagobert* than on the *Blue Moon*.

On the King's ship there was little friendliness but fine discipline. The cabin boys were bossed around by the sailors. The sailors were bossed around by the officers. The officers were bossed around by the Captain.

And quite a different leader from Philippe the Daring was this dandy Captain Bombon. His ruff was spotlessly clean. He wore a fine white wig between his bald head and his three-cornered hat. A fragrant odor of lily-of-the-valley warned everyone of his approach, because he dabbed himself with perfume.

"Sink that old pirate hull," he ordered his officers. "Send it to Neptune's sea chest. We will be handsomely rewarded by the King for capturing this wicked Philippe the Daring."

"Sink that old pirate hull," the officers ordered the sailors. "Somebody will be rewarded for your capture of the pirate leader."

"Aye, aye, sir," the sailors replied, although they well knew who would be rewarded.

They armed themselves with axes. They cut the ropes that bound the *Blue Moon* to the *Dagobert*. They chopped holes in the pirate ship. Slowly it sank into the sea.

"Moo," bawled Hortense, because it was past milking time and it looked as if she could no longer depend upon Philippe the Daring.

The spirited Countess had been bowed off to the best cabin high on the poop. Philippe the Daring was in chains below. The fleeing pirates had rowed out of sight.

When Madame Captain heard Hortense's forlorn bawl, she gave her another kick, then raised her horns high. "Moo," she ordered in a cross voice.

A cabin boy quickly appeared with a stool and bucket. First he sat and milked Madame Captain. She rolled her eyes. From time to time she slapped the boy in the face with the switch of her tail. When the poor lad was finished and about to pick up the bucket, Madame Captain lifted her hind leg and gave it a kick. The milk spilled over the deck.

It was fortunate that Hortense was there. The boy squatted on the stool again and began patiently milking her.

Madame Captain held her nose in the air. She was aware of her high rank. On the King's ship, the cow's milk went to no one but the Captain. The pigs provided pork and trotters for no one but the Captain. The hens laid eggs for the Captain alone. No wonder Madame Captain thought she had been born with a silver cud in her mouth.

"Moo," she bawled scornfully, because she wanted the new cow to know that she was no better than the common sailors in their blue-and-white striped suits, wide black hats, and buckled shoes.

"I am a captain's cow, and I have been around the Cape of Good Hope four times," she might have told Hortense.

And Hortense might have replied, "I am only a motherly Norman cow who fell into bad company through no fault of her own."

But neither cow said another moo, although the pigs squealed together in a comradely way and the hens gossiped back and forth while the rooster listened. They all seemed content with life in the manger—as that part of a ship is still called because the animals were kept by the anchor chain.

Hortense had not given up hope of finding her calf. A cow does not give up easily as any farmer knows. Neither fences nor green pastures can hold a cow forever if she thinks she wants to be loose.

Hortense made up her mind that Madame Captain was unfriendly because the white calf was hidden on the *Dagobert*. Perhaps Madame Captain didn't want Hortense to find the calf. Perhaps she wanted to keep the beautiful little one for herself.

Hortense bawled sadly and pulled at her rope halter. She wanted to look for her calf. She wanted to duck down the hatchway and look all around the hold. She wanted to climb the steps to the poop and look in all the cabin doors and windows. She wanted to climb to the crow's nest as she had seen so many sailors do. Something was up there, else why were the sailors always climbing the ropes?

Sometimes Hortense could see and smell the Captain strut out on the deck and look through a long spyglass. She wished that she could look through it. Perhaps she would see her long-lost calf.

As the *Dagobert* tacked northward, Madame Captain became more and more disagreeable. She began stealing hay from Hortense.

Poor Hortense! She knew hunger again. She was so very hungry that she began eying the rope that held her to the manger. She took it between her grinders and began chewing. It was tough but had a pleasant salty taste.

She chewed and waved the switch of her tail. This rope would probably make a tough cud, but a hungry cow could not be particular.

Then something happened that made Hortense forget the salty rope and her three hungry stomachs. Something happened that Captain Bombon could not order to do this or that. It must have begun like this.

Deep in his green castle at the bottom of the sea, the real King Neptune was holding court. He was an angry king. The fishes and shellbacks had brought him word about the goings-on aboard the *Blue Moon*.

"So they make fun of me," roared King Neptune. And his words shook the waves and quickened the winds. "A fat rascal with his face hidden behind seaweed dares to imitate me. They set up a clumsy cow as my beautiful queen. I will show them what happens when the real King Neptune boards a ship."

The fierce old King of the Deep called forth all of his scaly, popeyed subjects. He called forth his fellow rulers of the four winds. After all, the crime had taken place in their territory.

"Punish them!" roared King Neptune. "Sink their impudent ship!"

"It has already been sunk, Your Wet Majesty," said a mermaid. "I am living in it now."

"Somebody must be punished," cried the King. "Sink another ship. Sink every ship in African waters!"

The winds blew and howled. The skies darkened and

lowered. The sea rolled and churned. And all the powers of air and water attacked the King's ship *Dagobert*.

"I've never seen such a storm since that typhoon off the Indies," shouted Captain Bombon. "Reef the sails! Steer clear of those rocky shoals!"

The officers ran back and forth among the sailors. The sailors ran back and forth over the deck and up and down the rigging. The cabin boys wept with homesickness and groaned with seasickness. The Countess closed herself in her cabin and said her last prayers.

The pigs squealed in terror. They had looked forward to ending up as juicy chops and fat trotters. They didn't want to be wasted by drowning.

The chickens squawked and crowded around their frightened rooster for protection.

"Moo," bawled Hortense fearfully.

But Madame Captain raised her horns into the storm. She thought that nothing could happen to *her* because she was the Captain's cow.

Alas for captains and their cows and their ships when King Neptune is the enemy!

Despite the efforts of the King's sailors, the *Dagobert* was washed onto the shoals. There was a terrible crash. The decks trembled with fright and the masts shook.

"Moo," bawled Hortense, pulling at the rope, which she had chewed to a string.

"Swing out the boats," shouted the Captain to the officers. "We must abandon ship."

"Swing out the boats," shouted the officers to the sailors.

"Help swing out the boats," shouted the sailors to the cabin boys. But the cabin boys were already crouching in the boats.

The sailors swung out the boats and filled them with necessaries.

The Countess hurried from her cabin and was helped into a boat.

"Philippe the Daring," she reminded the King's captain. "You must save him."

"Indeed I must," said Captain Bombon, "or the King will never believe I captured the cutthroat. Bring up Philippe the Daring and put him in a boat," he ordered his officers.

"Bring up Philippe the Daring and put him in a boat," the officers ordered the sailors.

"Moo," bawled Hortense so they would remember her, too, because she was in water up to her hocks.

Captain Bombon heard her. She reminded him that his own cow was in danger.

"Women and cows first!" he cried to his officers. "Put my cow in my own boat."

Madame Captain was quickly untied and led away. But the pigs and chickens and Hortense were left to save themselves.

"Moo," bawled Hortense, crying for help again.

The Countess heard her, but it was too late. A giant wave washed over the sinking ship and carried the pigs away on a plank. The chickens sailed off in their coop.

The boats were washed away from the ship. The *Dagobert* slowly turned on its side with a shudder and a groan. As it did so, Hortense's string of a rope snapped in two. She went skidding on her pinbones the width of the deck. She somersaulted into the salty water.

"Moo," she started to bawl, but, like the rogues at King Neptune's make-believe court, her head was ducked under water.

She kicked her hoofs and raised her horns as high as Madame Captain's. She began swimming for the rocky shore. King Neptune, seeing the struggling cow, must have tried his best to hold her.

"That's the biggest rogue of all," he must have shouted. "She dared to impersonate my beautiful queen."

But Hortense fought out of his grasp. She felt hard rock under her feet. She pulled herself up on the rough beach. How could she know that she was stepping ashore in wildest Africa when she was only an unlettered Norman cow?

5.

Hortense's first impression of Africa was not a good one. She climbed a rugged cliff. She looked over barren, scrubby hills to high, forbidding mountains. She thought that never had she seen such poor pasture land. Only one other thought under her white poll kept her going. Perhaps her calf was lost in this forsaken land.

Africa was hot. It was hot as the village oven on baking day.

Hortense was thirsty. Worst of all, she had missed a milking.

In the dry gullies and scrubby hills she could not see a sign of a human being. Where were the peasants and the low, thatched barns? Where were all the cows and sheep and chickens? Where was her poor white calf?

Perhaps over that brown hill ahead. There was a faint trail like a lost cowpath circling it. She doggedly followed the trail. She followed it through deep passes and over dreary plains. She kept looking ahead eagerly.

Suddenly she stopped. She had seen something move in the bushes ahead. It must be her lost calf. She trotted along faster than ever. Her big soft eyes were drawn to the moving brush ahead.

Then a strange animal leaped out in front of her. Hortense had never seen such a beast. It looked like a cat that had never stopped growing. It had a thick black mane and a fat switch on the end of its tail. It had blazing eyes and long, curved claws. When it roared, its mouth showed great, yellow teeth.

Hortense was glad that she was not a mouse. Of course, she had never seen a lion before. She stopped stock-still on the trail. She lowered her horns and stared at the black-maned lion.

"Gr-r-r!" roared the lion as if he really meant it. He stared back at her. He had chased a graceful gazelle down from the mountains, and he was astonished to find her so misshapen from her struggles to escape. She no longer looked tender and appetizing. He growled with disappointment and lashed his sides with his tail. He turned around and disappeared into the underbrush.

Hortense was disappointed, too. She began walking again. She was walking somewhere, and she was anxious to get to that somewhere as fast as possible.

The dry, thorny trail led into a jagged valley. And near the end of it, Hortense smelled water. She mooed happily and began trotting. There was a water hole ahead of her. Most wonderful of all, there were men and beasts drinking from it.

But such men and beasts had never been seen in Normandy —not even at the fairs! The beasts had long goose necks and, most amazing of all, great humps on their backs. The men were dark brown and wore flowing white robes.

"Moo," bawled Hortense happily, because a thirsty, un-milked cow is never particular.

The dark men were surprised to see Hortense. One of them raised a long curved sword, but another beckoned him to put it away. They slowly and cautiously approached Hortense. They pointed at her hoofs and horns.

"Not a camel," said one man in awe.

"Not a gazelle," said another.

"Moo," bawled Hortense, because she already knew this. She had never pretended to be a camel or a gazelle.

The men walked all around her. They pointed at her pin-bones and the switch on her tail.

"An impossible animal," they decided.

Then one of them saw that Hortense needed milking badly. "One stands up to milk a camel," he said. "How does one milk an animal that is not a camel?"

They argued and argued about this. One of them went for a goatskin bag to catch the milk in. At last an Arab lay on his back under Hortense, and she milked quite well that way, although it had never been tried before.

When the milking was done, the men took turns staring into the goatskin bag.

"Milk," they said in surprise, as if they had expected to

see honey or soup.

Then they allowed Hortense to go to the water hole. She stepped in between two camels. "Moo?" she asked politely.

One camel looked down at her scornfully. Then it spat at her. The other camel looked down at her even more scornfully. It lowered its goose neck and gave her a sharp bite on the back.

"Moo," bawled Hortense, who was not used to such rudeness in her own placid Norman herd.

The two camels lifted their haughty heads higher than Madame Captain had ever held her horns. They walked away from the water hole swaying their hips grandly. Camels are very stupid. Only stupid creatures think that they are better than those whose looks and ways are different from their own.

Hortense spread her hoofs apart and thrust her dry nose into the water. She drank and drank and drank. She drank until her skin would hardly hold her together.

Then she studied the camels. They were chewing cuds, too. But they did not chew from side to side. They chewed back and forth and up and down all at once. Hortense was sure they were cows now—great hump-backed, goose-necked cows.

The dark men called out commands to the camels. One by one the beasts dropped to their knees. They folded their

61

hind legs under them. All the while, they moaned and groaned with complaints. The men paid no heed. They mounted the shaggy humps. They cried more commands. The camels rose on their long, crooked legs. They grunted as if they were dying.

"Moo," bawled Hortense. She had made a mistake. These beasts were not cows. They were horses. Tatata! Such horses had never been seen in Normandy.

Hortense was roped to one of the unfriendly camels. She began a long march. All the way to the Arab camp she watched the camels' big, spongy toes and their frayed tails and goose rumps.

The Arab camp was made of tents. Black-eyed women and children ran out to meet the men. Three mangy dogs ran out, too. They raced to Hortense. They snuffed at her and bared their fangs. Oh, there was nothing strange about

these dogs. Normandy was full of them.

Hortense lowered her horns and shook them. The snarling, barking dogs behaved much like the lion. They ran away. Instead of thrashing their tails against their sides, they squeezed them between their legs.

The camels were separated. Each was taken before his master's tent. A front leg was hobbled to a hind one. The same thing was done to Hortense.

"Moo," bawled Hortense, feeling that this was an indignity. Cows that jumped fences had wooden collars put around their necks, and pigs that rooted in the garden had rings put in their noses. But Hortense had never jumped fences nor rooted in gardens.

In the early morning, just as in Normandy, the milking was done. Hortense was milked with the camels. The ugly beasts turned up their noses and lowered their eyelids as the men stood up to milk them. To a cow from Normandy, this was an unusual sight.

Hortense was herded with the camels. A man drove them to a high plain to graze for the day.

Poor grazing it was! The stupid camels were content to chew thorny bushes. Hortense had to search all through the brush to fill even one of her stomachs.

She grew thinner and thinner every day. Her pinbones were almost as sharp as the thorns upon which the camels fed.

Her four-legged companions acted as if she did not exist at all. They had never seen an antelope with such horns nor a goat so large. They were sure that there was no such animal as Hortense.

But the cow knew that she existed. Her three hungry stomachs told her so. The hot sun told her so. She toiled over the rough earth in her search for food because she wanted to go on existing.

She was lonely, so she tried to make friends with the camels again. They only spat at her and stuck out their lower lips.

Poor, lonely Hortense! She was sure that there was no hope of finding her white calf among such enemies.

One day there was great bustle and excitement in the Arab camp. Hortense heard a tumult of bells and hoofs and shouting. She raised her horns with curiosity because she had learned that anything—just anything at all—can appear in Africa.

The cow was not disappointed. A strange caravan approached the camp. It was made up of four donkeys. On the first one rode a queer little man who did not look like an Arab nor a Frenchman. He looked like no one but himself. His long, stringy hair fell from under a floppy hat. His face was bony as Hortense's rump. He wore a long Arab robe that reached all the way to his wooden shoes. And over his head he held a black umbrella.

The donkeys were loaded down with water bags and sacks of dirt. One looked quite gay because his burden was a great basket of plants and flowers. It was as if this strange

little man carried his farm with him.

The Arabs, their children, and all their dogs ran out to meet the stranger. They did not know if he came as friend or enemy.

The little man bowed from his seat on the donkey. He spoke to them in their own language.

"Peace be with you, my brothers," he said. "I am Master Dadou, botanist and explorer."

The Arabs looked toward their sheik. He returned the stranger's greeting. "Peace, brother," he said. "Our home is your home."

Master Dadou dismounted. He anxiously went to the basket of plants and flowers. He carefully sprinkled them from a water bag. "Patience, my little friends," he said to them.

"Moo," bawled Hortense, because the green growing things made her hungry. The botanist saw her for the first time. The donkeys saw her for the first time, too. They lifted their long ears and laughed in a chorus.

"Hee, haw! Hee, haw! Hee, haw!" laughed all the donkeys as if Hortense was the funniest sight they had seen in Africa.

"What kind of beast is this?" the stranger asked the Arabs. Of course, if he had seen Hortense in France, he would have known at once that she was a cow. But he was seeing her in a part of Africa where there were no cows.

"It has no name," said the Sheik.

"There is no such animal," said the camel-herder proudly.

Master Dadou grew excited. This must be a rare beast indeed. No one had ever heard of one before.

He walked all around Hortense. He looked at her sharp pinbones and her sharp hip bones. He looked at her curving horns.

"A gnu," he decided at last. "A most rare beast. I have never seen one before myself."

"Hee, haw, hee, haw," laughed the donkeys as if a gnu was just too ridiculous.

Master Dadou went to his donkey mount and pulled a notebook from a pack. He wrote in it:

THIS DAY SAW A GNU FOR THE FIRST TIME.

IT HAS HORNS LIKE A COW AND A BODY LIKE A

COW. IT IS A VERY STRANGE BEAST.

The Arabs wanted to know more about Master Dadou and his business. As they sat around the campfire eating camel stew, the Sheik asked the explorer, "Why have you come to our country?"

"To win the favor of my king," answered Master Dadou.

The Sheik was more bewildered than ever. "And how do you hope to win the favor of your king unless you are fighting for him?"

"My king loves exotic plants for his palace garden," explained the botanist. "So I have tramped over Africa getting them for him."

"Who is your king?" asked the Sheik. "Is he the Sultan of Morocco?"

"The French king, of course," said Master Dadou. "What other king matters?"

"Does he live in the wooden houses that float on the sea?" asked the Sheik.

"Dear, no," said Master Dadou. "Those are ships. He lives in a great palace on the other side of the world."

The Arabs looked at each other unbelievingly. The Sheik said, "There is no other side to the world. The desert is the whole world."

"Indeed it is not," exclaimed the botanist. "It is a very small part of the world."

"Moo," interrupted Hortense, because she knew the botanist was right. Once she had thought that her village in Normandy was all the world.

The Sheik narrowed his eyes cunningly. "Is the sun in your land—and the moon and stars?" he asked.

"Of course," said Master Dadou.

The Sheik frowned. "You are lying," he said. "The sun and the moon and the stars are here, so how can they be in another land?"

Then the donkeys started laughing again. "Hee, haw, hee, haw," they laughed.

The botanist tried to be patient. "Where are your moon and stars now?" he asked the Arabs.

No one could answer the question. When the sun sank behind the hills, the botanist asked, "Where is your sun now?"

"It goes to sleep in the sea," said the Sheik.

Then Master Dadou was so put out that he began to talk to himself in his own language. Hortense pricked up her ears. It seemed so long since she had heard anyone speak French. It had been so long since she had seen green plants and flowers.

"Moo," she bawled with homesickness for the green fields of Normandy.

Master Dadou quickly opened his notebook and wrote:

A GNU MAKES A NOISE LIKE A COW, TOO.

6.

Hortense was so homesick that she could not sleep that night.

At dawn Master Dadou packed his donkeys again. He watered the plants again. Then he turned to the Sheik. "My king is also interested in exotic beasts," he said, "and keeps a zoo of them at his palace. I will give you four gold pieces for the gnu."

The Sheik answered, "Our beasts are our gold," he said, "and we do not keep them in a zoo."

Master Dadou was disappointed. "I am sure she would win the favor of the King for me," he said.

"Why do you wish your king's favor?" asked the Sheik. "Don't you have a tent to shade your body and food to fill your stomach?"

"Everyone wants to win the King's favor," said the botanist. "They try to do it by going to his court and saying clever things. But my only hope is to please him with my gifts from Nature."

The Sheik shook his head in a puzzled manner. "Such a strange king," he said. "But we will not sell our gnu."

Master Dadou ate his disappointment and made his polite farewells. Then he straddled one of the donkeys. He raised his umbrella. He kicked the donkey's sides. The caravan of donkeys started marching. Although heavily burdened, they walked with dainty, mincing steps.

Hortense watched them go.

"Moo," she cried with all her homesickness.

When the camel-herder unhobbled her and drove her to pasture with the camels, she could hear the hee, haw of the donkeys on the trail below.

Then Hortense did a sly thing for a cow. She slowly ate herself away from the camels and the herder. She ate herself into the low, dry bushes. She ate herself down the trail.

Hortense suddenly stopped eating. She picked up her hoofs and her tail and began galloping toward the donkey caravan. The man who spoke French would surely lead her to her calf.

Through the dry gullies she charged, horns down and tail flying. Only a gazelle could have passed her.

She caught up with the donkey caravan.

"The gnu," cried Master Dadou in surprise, as he watched Hortense come charging across a plain. He pulled out his

notebook. Despite his donkey's swaying, he was able to write:

A GNU IS ONE OF THE FLEETEST BEASTS IN ALL AFRICA.

Hortense stopped her gallop. She peacefully followed the donkeys. She liked the way they walked so mincingly on their dainty little ankles. She tried to walk that way herself, but the sand got between her hoofs and her hocks ached.

The sun beat down so hotly that Master Dadou held the umbrella over the plants and flowers instead of himself. Every little while he stopped and gave them more water.

"Patience, my little friends," he implored them.

He gave the donkeys and Hortense water, too. He even drank some himself because the heat was so great.

Then on they trudged across the sandy waste.

Suddenly Hortense's glazed eyes were delighted to see a wonderful sight ahead. Master Dadou was really leading her back to Normandy, for there before her weary eyes lay a Norman village. Tall, green trees grew by a blue lake. Low Norman cottages stood among the trees.

Hortense couldn't wait to get to her village. She gave a last spurt forward. She ran in front of the donkeys. She hurried to the village. She wanted to bathe her hot hoofs in the blue lake and drink its blue waters.

Then, as suddenly as the village had appeared, it disappeared into thin, hot desert air. It was only a mirage.

"Moo," bawled Hortense pitifully.

The donkeys thought the joke the desert had played on Hortense was the funniest yet. "Hee, haw, hee, haw," they laughed.

Hortense dropped her horns in shame while they went past her. She fell into place in the rear. She walked until she was ready to drop into the sand.

When another village appeared ahead, she paid no attention to it. Even when the donkeys led her into a grove of palm trees, she was sure the oasis would disappear like the Norman village.

The desert oasis did not disappear. It stayed around her. She and the donkeys had all the water they could drink. So did the plants and flowers. And Master Dadou filled all the water bags, which had been emptied so fast on the hot desert. He filled some of them with the milk he took from Hortense.

The botanist was pleased that Hortense had chosen to follow him. He wrote in his notebook:

ALTHOUGH GNUS ARE VERY FIERCE IN THEIR NATURAL STATE, THEY ARE EASILY TAMED. THEIR MILK TASTES MUCH LIKE THAT OF A COW.

But the donkeys were no friendlier than the camels. They whispered jokes about Hortense, then laughed like hyenas.

Although Hortense's feelings were hurt, she tried not to show it. All the way across the desert stretch and through the mountains to the white seaport town, the cow pretended to take no notice of the laughing donkeys.

She followed them down steep, narrow streets, where dark men stared at them and women had nothing but eyes on their faces.

In the square, camels and noisy natives crowded around the well. Master Dadou was puzzled to see some bullocks and their skinny cows. He looked from them to Hortense. He wrote in his notebook:

GNUS ARE NOT RARE IN SOME PARTS OF AFRICA.

They did not tarry any longer than necessary at the Moorish well. The natives were unfriendly to Master Dadou, and the camels, as usual, were unfriendly to Hortense. The bullocks and the cows glared at her as if she were some distant cousin who had turned up uninvited.

The botanist led his beasts down a steep street to the harbor. The hot sun shone on the blue sea and the small ships with their bright sails.

"This looks familiar," Hortense must have thought to herself.

It seemed even more familiar when she and the donkeys were driven across a gangway and stepped into one of the small ships.

The old roll of the sea was familiar to her three stomachs, too. But the crew was different. They spoke in many languages and pushed and shoved one another.

Hortense thought about her first sea voyage. She thought about Philippe the Daring and the spirited Countess. She thought about the wild onions.

She couldn't stop thinking about the wild onions. Master Dadou's flowers made her think about them because they smelled so different.

The baskets of plants and bags of dirt were lined up on the deck. Master Dadou fussed about them as if they were his helpless children.

"No, no, little ones, you must not droop so," he tried to cheer them. "Lift your heads to the sea breezes. See, I give you a drink of water so you will not feel so sad. And if I run out of water, you shall have milk."

Something so wonderful happened in his basket garden that he scribbled in his notebook for almost an hour. He did not write one word about gnus. He began by writing:

THE RARE YELLOW ORCHID HAS BLOOMED AT LAST.

The rakish members of the crew could not help taking an interest in his little garden. Hortense was even more interested. Especially since the dry straw given to her and the donkeys was so tasteless. She liked the yellow orchid. It looked to her like a cowslip in a green meadow.

It is not at all surprising that the first time the botanist turned his back, she began sampling the contents of the basket. For the King of France indeed! Only a hungry cow could really appreciate these rare plants.

She saved the orchid for the last because it had a beautiful dessert look. It was as good as it looked. A little salt might have brought out its flavor, but who thinks to put salt on an orchid?

"Hee, haw, hee, haw," laughed the donkeys when they saw the horrified look on the botanist's face. As long as it wasn't their hay Hortense had eaten, they thought it very funny.

First Master Dadou was going to throw them into the sea for their laughter. Then he was going to throw Hortense into the sea. At last he decided to throw himself in.

"My life is ruined," he cried, tearing his stringy hair. "My career is ruined. I will never become a court favorite."

But the Moorish captain would not let him throw himself into the sea.

"Who will take care of the beasts and milk the gnu?" he grumbled. "My crew has enough work to do."

Then the botanist thought of a new reason for living. Besides, the sea was so deep.

"That is right," he said. "Who will take care of the gnu? Who will lead her to the King? Who will be made keeper of the royal gardens for giving the King his first gnu?"

"Hee, haw, hee, haw," the donkeys laughed.

But the joke was on them because Master Dadou sold all of them but one to a farmer when he landed in France.

"They have a great sense of humor," he told the farmer.

"I buy donkeys to carry my grain to the mill," said the

farmer, "not to amuse me."

Master Dadou mounted his only remaining donkey. Leading Hortense by a rope he set out for the King's palace at Versailles.

The cow felt the long trip must be almost over by now. The world could not be much bigger. She had seen most of it but had not found her calf yet. The white calf must be in that small part of the world she had not yet visited.

All the way to the King's palace at Versailles, the trio passed farm villages and fields filled with cows. Master Dadou would look at the cows in a puzzled way as if he, too, had never seen them before.

He would read the notes he had written in Africa. He would look at Hortense and talk to himself. "I must reason this out," he explained to himself. "If a beast is a gnu in Africa, it must still be a gnu if it is brought to France. It could not change from a gnu to a cow during a voyage. That is reasonable. That is scientific." But he kept looking uneasily at Hortense.

7.

Never had Hortense seen such beautiful palaces and spacious parks. Certainly she had never seen them on the African desert. The trees and flowers alone were enough to make a thin, hungry cow's mouth water.

Of course, Hortense did not know that she was in royal Versailles. She did not know that these grand properties belonged to Louis XVI and his queen, Marie Antoinette. She was a humble peasant cow who had never expected to see royal palaces.

Master Dadou felt very proud and important. He met a nobleman being carried in a sedan chair. He boldly asked where the King might be found. "I am bringing him a rare beast from Africa," he explained.

The courtier looked at Hortense and smiled behind his jeweled hand. "The Queen has more of a fancy for that kind of rare beast," he answered. "Take her to the Petit Trianon. The next path will lead you there."

Master Dadou was grateful for the nobleman's help. "Already I am learning court intrigue," he said to himself. "One wins the King through the Queen."

"Moo," said Hortense, whose only intrigue had been the tricky way in which she had run away from the camel herd.

They followed the pleasant path that seemed in no hurry to get where it was going. It went through a deep forest, taking its own time.

Then Hortense saw a sight that made her almost giddy with delight. There beyond her dazzled eyes lay a blue lake. Slim willows wept green tears into its smooth waters. White swans sailed on its mirror. Along its half circle was a cluster of peasant cottages. It was a village more beautiful than any she had ever seen in Normandy.

As they approached the village, they passed peasants leading sheep by long blue ribbons. A flock of white doves flew over Hortense's horns.

Somewhere she had seen this blue and green village before. She was so eager to get to it that she rushed ahead of the donkey.

"Baa," said the sheep in a friendly way. "Coo," said a dove tenderly as it perched on her horn for a moment's rest.

Then Hortense remembered where she had seen this village before. It had been the mirage on the desert. The wood-land village with its blue lake and friendly sheep and doves would disappear, too. Perhaps she and the botanist and the silly donkey would find themselves back in bleak Africa.

She stopped and let the donkey take the lead again.

But the village did not disappear. They went along its winding path. Hortense saw that, although the thatched cottages looked old, the cracks had been newly painted on their walls. And each had a garden bursting with flowers and fruit trees.

The peasants were neater and cleaner than any she had seen in Normandy. They were certainly cleaner than any Arabs she had seen in Africa.

"A cow," cried one of them, leaning over the picket fence. "Just a brown and white cow. Why does the Queen want such a common-looking cow?"

"Moo," bawled Hortense in protest. Perhaps she was trying to tell the peasant that she was a most uncommon cow. As for queens, she had been one herself with a diamond necklace around her throat and fashionable curls on her horns.

Master Dadou did not like the peasant's words either. He scowled at the man. "Have you never seen a gnu?" he asked, as if they were to be seen every day.

The peasant stared stolidly at Hortense. "No," he answered, "but I've seen cows."

Suddenly there was a tinkle of laughter from the winding outdoor stairway of one of the cottages. Some young women came skipping down the steps. They were even more charming in looks than the other peasants. They wore white muslin gowns with wide blue sashes. Prettiest among them was a tall girl with deep blue eyes. In her golden hair were twined white flowers from the exotic potato plant that had come from far-off America.

The pretty girl looked from Hortense to the donkey. "Which are you bringing to the farm?" she asked. "The cow or the donkey? Or both? There are really enough cows. Perhaps the donkey—"

Master Dadou was quite put out with her. "You peasants are ignoramuses," he fumed. "This is not a cow, my simple maiden. For the first time a gnu is to be seen in Europe."

The other girls started to speak all at once, but the golden-haired girl silenced them. "Which is the gnu?" she asked.

"The cow is the gnu," said the botanist testily. "I mean the gnu is the cow. Oh, heaven help my waggling tongue! I mean that the cow isn't a cow at all. She is a gnu."

"Moo," bawled Hortense, because she was a motherly Nor-

man cow who had never pretended to be anything she was not.

"Unfortunately she has eaten all the African plants I was bringing for His Majesty's garden," continued Master Dadou.

"Then let her eat cake," said the pretty girl.

A red-haired peasant girl came out of a door. "I will go with all of you," she said, "although I simply can't learn to milk a—"

She stopped abruptly at sight of Master Dadou and his beasts.

There was something familiar about the girl. When she came closer, Hortense immediately recognized the Countess wearing her hair flat on her head.

"Moo," bawled Hortense as if to say, "Don't you remember me?"

The Countess recognized her voice. "Why if it isn't Hortense, the village cow!" she exclaimed. "Such unusual people as one meets at court!"

"Moo," bawled Hortense, because she thought that was true of Normandy or of Africa.

Master Dadou was red as a turkey cock. "Stupid peasant!" he cried. "I am Master Dadou, the great botanist and explorer, and I wish an audience with the Queen of France."

The golden-haired girl smiled mischievously. "You are

having it, Master Dadou," she said. "I am the Queen of France."

The botanist's eyes popped, and his hands trembled. Oh, he was a poor master of court intrigue! At his first royal audience, he had played the country chaw-bacon.

In his haste to dismount respectfully, he fell off the donkey. The girls giggled at the ridiculous sight of the botanist lying flat at the Queen's feet.

"Hee, haw, hee, haw," cried the donkey, having his last laugh.

"No one bows to me here," the Queen said to the man gently. "I am a rustic milkmaid today."

The unhappy man struggled to his wooden shoes. "Forgive me, Your Majesty—Your Most Rustic Majesty," he begged. "The sun of Africa has addled my brains."

"You are forgiven," said the Queen graciously. "Now tell me about your wonderful beast."

"She is an African gnu," said Master Dadou, feeling more like himself again. "She is truly an extraordinary beast."

"Of course Hortense is extraordinary," put in the Countess. "If she should ever decide to write her memories, my good man, they would be worth reading."

The Queen was puzzled. "How do I know this is not a gnu if I have never seen a gnu?" she asked.

The Countess told how to solve the riddle. "Let our friend, the Admiral, settle this," she said. "He knows Hortense, too."

"Send for the Admiral," ordered the royal milkmaid. "He is at the Trianon with my husband."

"Bring the Admiral," cried all the pretty girls. "He is so charming."

So the peasants who looked more like peasants hurried away to fetch the charming Admiral.

Master Dadou flustered and blustered. He was beginning to feel like an old hand at court intrigue.

"Your Majesty," he boasted, "little do you know of the dangers that beset me in capturing this gnu. Anyone knows that the gnu is the fiercest beast in all Africa. There I was without a gun or sword when this gnu cornered me in a ravine."

"Moo," bawled Hortense in reproach.

"The beast charged," continued Master Dadou, "bellowing like a bull and grunting like a rhinoceros. And there I was at its mercy."

All the time Master Dadou was taking the parts first of himself and then of the mad gnu, Hortense looked at him with big, sad eyes. She knew that she had never committed violence. And the Countess stood with her hands on her hips and smiled as scornfully as a camel.

"How did you escape death?" asked Marie Antoinette. "Do tell us."

Master Dadou made a heroic attempt to get himself out of the ravine. He looked at Hortense desperately, as if she had cornered him again. Then he remembered how he had saved himself from her.

"I suddenly remembered that in my pack was a rare yellow orchid," he went on. "Of all plants, there is none a gnu likes as much as a yellow orchid. I grabbed the orchid and held it under her nose. And she grew gentle as a lamb."

"Moo," bawled Hortense, because she had never heard such a fairy tale.

Master Dadou felt triumphant. He spread his feet apart and clasped his hands behind his back. He imagined himself clad in silk and laces and wearing powder in his long, stringy hair.

Then the Admiral arrived. The Admiral did not look like

a peasant or a courtier. Despite his gold braid and ruffles, he looked like nothing so much as a pirate. The curly black beard growing anyhow and every which way did not match the white wig.

"Moo," bawled Hortense in happy recognition of Philippe the Daring. She thought the world a very small place after all—almost as small as the Arabs believed it.

"Hortense, the sailor cow," exclaimed the Admiral. "Ah, what happy memories she brings me of my carefree days!"

The Countess smirked. "The King gave you the choice of being hanged as a pirate or of commanding his fleet as an admiral," she reminded him. "Aren't you happy?"

Philippe the Daring shrugged his golden shoulders. "What choice could I make?" he asked. "There are more old admirals than old pirates."

"Moo," bawled Hortense, because the talk was turned from the question of whether she was a cow or a gnu. But the royal milkmaid had not forgotten.

"This is all so confusing," she said. "We will take this beast to meet my cows, Blanchette and Brunette. Cows should be the best experts on cows."

So Hortense was led to the little stone barn among the trees. In the neat stable two cows were placidly munching their clean, sweet hay. One of them was dark and shiny as mahogany. The other was white as milk.

Blanchette, the white cow, raised her milky head. She stared at the newcomer. Then she gave a long, tender bawl. "Moo-o-o!" she bawled happily.

Hortense's soft eyes filled with tears. "Moo," she answered back.

She broke away from Master Dadou and rushed to Blanchette. She licked her white poll and shoulders. She nuzzled her tenderly.

"They seem to know each other," said the Queen.

"Your Majesty, they are mother and daughter," confessed the Countess. "You have been told that Blanchette is a Swiss cow, but she really comes from my own village in Normandy."

"Moo," bawled Hortense, because she thought it was time that somebody told the truth.

Marie Antoinette's own eyes filled with tears at the sight of this touching reunion of mother and daughter. She was a motherly person herself and dearly loved her own little children.

"But why did you say that she was a gnu?" she turned to ask Master Dadou.

The botanist did not hear her. He had walked outside and mounted his donkey. He was busily writing in his notebook:

A COW IS A COW ANYWHERE.

Then he clucked to his donkey and turned his back upon court intrigue forever.

"Moo," bawled Hortense, because it was past her milking time again.

"Bring me my little stool and my alabaster vase," commanded Marie Antoinette.

As she milked Hortense, all of her noble companions stared into the vase with admiration. Never had they seen such rich, creamy milk. Then the pretty queen led them into the dairy with its marble tables. They churned butter, and the Queen rolled out golden pats of it with her own royal hands.

So Hortense's adventures ended in the most fitting way. The motherly Norman cow who had never pretended to be anything else became the favorite pet of a gay queen who loved to play that she was somebody else.